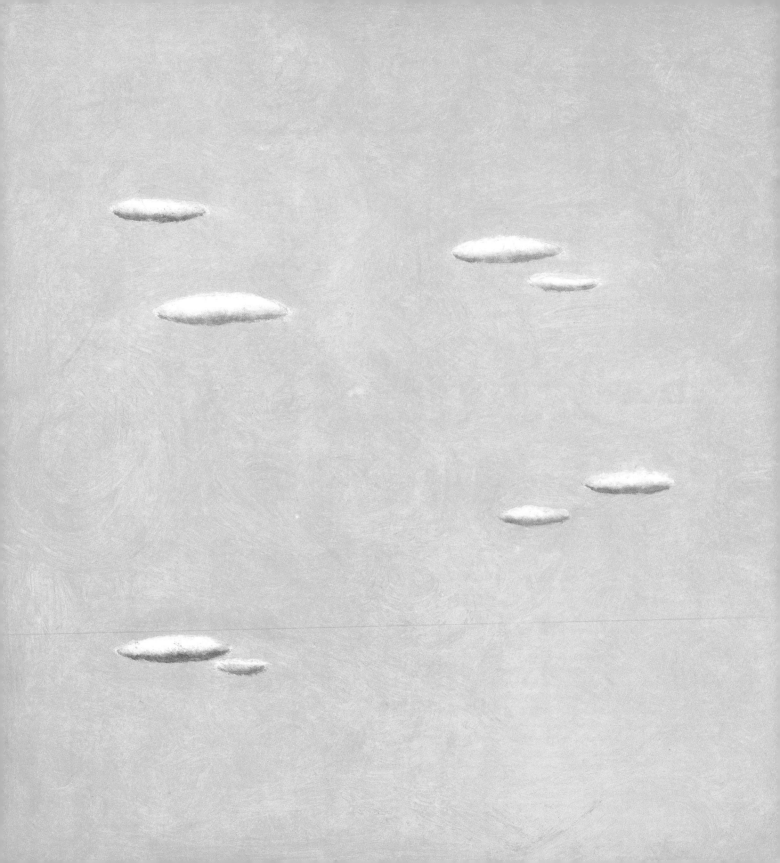

If Kisses Were Colors

JANET LAWLER * ILLUSTRATED BY ALISON JAY

DIAL BOOKS FOR YOUNG READERS ✦ NEW YORK

Published by Dial Books for Young Readers
A division of Penguin Young Readers Group
345 Hudson Street
New York, New York 10014
Text copyright © 2003 by Janet Lawler
Illustrations copyright © 2003 by Alison Jay
All rights reserved
Designed by Lily Malcom
Text set in Mrs. Eaves Italic
Manufactured in China on acid-free paper
7 9 10 8 6

Library of Congress Cataloging-in-Publication Data
Lawler, Janet.
If kisses were colors / Janet Lawler ; illustrated by Alison Jay.
p. cm.
Summary: A parent describes kisses in many
different ways, all of which express love for baby.
ISBN 0-8037-2617-1
[1. Kissing—Fiction. 2. Love—Fiction. 3. Parent and child—Fiction.
4. Stories in rhyme.] I. Jay, Alison, ill. II. Title.
PZ8.3.L355 If 2003
[E]—dc21
2002003978

*The art was created using alkyd oil paint
on paper with crackling varnish.*

For Andy and Cami
J.L.

For Anne with love
A.J.

If kisses
were colors . . .

If kisses were colors, you'd see every one

of the bands of a rainbow that shines in the sun.

If kisses were pebbles, your beach would be lined

with stones by the millions, of all shapes and kinds.

If kisses were comets, the sky would be bright

with flashes of fire that streak through the night.

If kisses were flowers, you'd have huge bouquets

of roses and daisies   picked fresh every day.

If kisses were raindrops, a sea would appear,

created by showers that fall far and near.

If kisses were acorns, a forest would grow

of beautiful oak trees, in row after row.

If kisses were snowflakes, your world would be light,

sparkling with crystals of silver and white.

If kisses were blankets,
you'd always be warm,

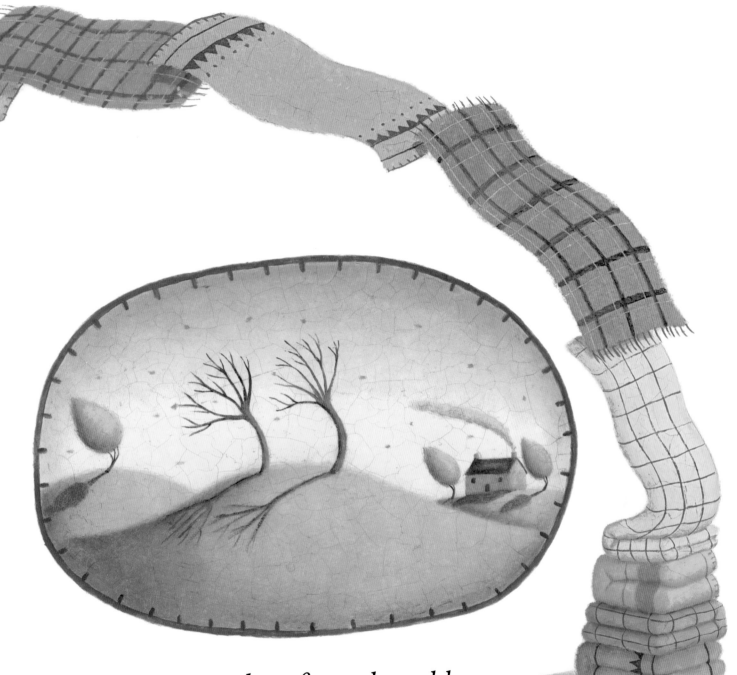

wrapped up from the cold
during winter's worst storm.

My kisses are colors, and raindrops that flow,

and pebbles, and acorns, and comets that glow,

and flowers, and snowflakes that fall from above;

they're my way, sweet baby,
to give you my love.